Lázaro Droznes

MY FAVORITE NAZI

The myth of Albert Speer; the good Nazi

Published by UNITEXTO

MY FAVORITE NAZI

The myth of Albert Speer; the good Nazi.

Two lecterns illuminated with overhead light in a typical courtroom with a black background. Enters Albert Speer, skinny, tall, round face, around 40 years and is located behind a lectern. He is nice and charismatic. The 40-year-old Prosecutor enters the opposite side, a robust complexion, dressed in a typical robe of the members of the judiciary.

FISCAL
Can you say your full name?

SPEER
Berthold Konrad Hermann Albert Speer

FISCAL
Whatever you will say from now on will be under oath.
Can you read this text?

The prosecutor hands a sheet of paper. Speer reads the sheet solemnly with one hand in the air showing the palm of his hand.

SPEER
I swear to God, the Almighty, Omnipresent and Omniscient, to tell the truth, the whole truth and nothing but the truth, without making additions or omissions with the purpose of modifying the perception of reality.

FISCAL
You are subject to trial under the following four charges:
1.Conspiracy to conduct a war of aggression 2. Crimes against peace 3. War crimes 4. Crimes against Humanity
How do you plead?

FISCAL
Not guilty.

FISCAL
What positions and functions did he have in the III Reich?

SPEER
Hitler's personal architect, Minister of arms production, General Inspector of Roads, General Inspector of Power Plants, Director of the Todt Organization...

FISCAL *(interrupting with annoyance).*
How many charges did you have?

SPEER
It's too long a list, around 12. I was also a Member of the *Reichstag*, that is the Parliament.

FISCAL
What relationship did you have with Adolf Hitler?

SPEER
Hitler did not have friends, but if he could, I would have been one of them. I was his personal architect, responsible for urban planning for the next 1000 years of the III Reich, the design and construction of the new *Chancellery*, the *Zeppelinfeld* in Nuremberg, many other buildings and also the Party rallies.

FISCAL
Have you ever been aware you were contributing with your architecture to build a criminal state?

SPEER
I always wanted to be an architect. I was not interested in politics. Nor was I interested in the political use of my

work. If necessary, I would have sold my soul to make great buildings, just like Faust. In Hitler I found my Mephistopheles. All he wanted is to dominate the world ... and I would design the buildings required for that purpose.

FISCAL
Do you admit that you sold your soul to the Devil?

SPEER
I wanted to be the architect of Germany, the best. I was trapped in terrible circumstances, with very few options, almost none. I could only forsake my conscience and move on.

FISCAL
You were not forced. You had options.

SPEER
I was living every architect's dream. Huge projects without any budget restrictions.

FISCAL
Many Germans refused to move on.

SPEER
I could not quit. I could not leave Germany. I'm too German ... *(pause)* I had to stay in Germany to prove my father was wrong... I must say that my father had always disqualified me as an architect.

FISCAL
When did you meet Hitler and under what circumstances?

SPEER
In December 1930 I attended an act of the Party at the

Berlin *Sportpalast*. I was magnetized by his words and I joined the Nazi party 3 months later. I always had great admiration for Hitler, until the war began.

FISCAL
You´re not the kind of person associated to the band that ruled Germany with Hitler. How did you relate to that intimate circle, so different?

SPEER
They never accepted me completely. I was not a bird of the same feather. They were forced to work with me. Even now in prison they don't accept me.

FISCAL
What was the true nature of your affinity with Hitler? What did you share?

SPEER
It was the passion for architecture. We worked many years in the redesign of Berlin to make it the most beautiful city in the world. We spend entire nights discussing ideas and models of the future capital city of Germania.

FISCAL
What is Germania?

SPEER
Germany, after the war, would be called Germania, the name for the hegemonic power. As was the United Kingdom in the 19th century, as was Rome for so many centuries. With Hitler we developed the concept of the ruin value: the great buildings had to be constructed in such a way that they would be aesthetically pleasing ruins

after thousands of years, as a testament to the greatness of the Third Reich. That way the Germania ruins would be seen in the future as we now see the Roman ruins.

FISCAL
What tasks did you have as First Commissioner of Nazi Party Buildings, your first official position?

SPEER
My mission was to ensure the uniformity of criteria in all Nazi party buildings. I had no connection to the war preparations. I didn't even know they existed.

FISCAL
You were responsible for the deportation of 30,000 Jews to liberate an area of Berlin for the purpose of urban redesign. What did you know about the fate of deported Jews?

SPEER
I didn't know anything. The fate of the Jews was a state secret. This matter was not discussed. One day I went through a train station and saw Jews waiting in line to be transported. I felt a great malaise, a feeling of very dark events looming ahead ... those feelings and thoughts faded away and I moved on.

FISCAL
Therefore, you knew, but didn't want to know.

SPEER
Most Germans did the same. I ignored everything that could hinder achieving my dreams.

FISCAL
As a minister, you used the rail system to ship raw

materials and military equipment. You should have known that the trains were busy with the transport of Jews.

SPEER

In Germany, nobody wanted to know anything that was not within his jurisdiction. I knew enough about the fate of the Jews to know I didn't want to know anything more.

FISCAL

You were more concerned with ambition than with the morality of your actions. How can you live with your conscience?

SPEER

I was very young, 26 years old. All I wanted is to be an architect, to get good projects, to be successful. To make my dreams come true.

FISCAL

That was true until the war began. What happened then?

SPEER

The dreams were over. When I entered the Cabinet as a minister in February 1942, my relationship with Hitler changed completely. Before, we were fellow architects discussing architecture issues we both loved. As Minister of the Cabinet I received direct orders from Hitler. I didn´t like the new nature of the relationship, but I had no alternative. I had to fulfill my obligations to Germany, my homeland.

FISCAL

Let's start with the charges. First, you are accused of conspiracy to carry out a war of aggression.

SPEER

Not true. Before becoming a minister, I dedicated myself to architecture. I had nothing to do with the decisions that led to war. I was engaged in urban planning in Berlin and Nuremberg. These activities had nothing to do with the organization of war, quite the opposite. They were impediments to war, as they required large amounts of raw materials, equipment and workers, which could otherwise be used directly or indirectly for rearmament. Moreover, these projects are only feasible in the long term and gave me the impression that Hitler was thinking of having a long period of peace that would allow us to execute the projects. Unfortunately, it was not so.

FISCAL

You knew from the book MY FIGHT about Hitler's aggressive plans towards the East and West countries, in particular towards the Soviet Union.

SPEER

No one took the political platform of MY FIGHT very seriously. We thought they were bravados to achieve power. Once in the Government, we all thought that logic and common sense would prevail.

FISCAL

But, you gave your consent to Hitler's decision to unleash an aggressive war. You remained a member of the party and participated in the war effort, by action or omission.

SPEER

A war of aggression can only be decided and executed by the person who has the supreme command. In a dictatorship like Hitler's, there was no conspiracy. We had all to obey Hitler, and his decision had the force of law. It was called the *Führerprinzip*. Obedience cannot be the subject of a criminal charge. In our country, there were millions of murders but no murderers, except one. All others were led and had to obey, although they have contributed significantly to the war effort. Consequently, the charge of carrying out a war of aggression does not apply.

FISCAL
You say you have no responsibility because you were subject to due obedience. You are in the same situation as a boy who kills his parents and then asks to be forgiven because he's an orphan

SPEER

All the Nazis were required to take the following oath: "I swear eternal faithfulness to Adolph Hitler. I swear unconditional obedience to Fuehrer and his government. "

FISCAL
By joining the Government, you have approved and accepted crimes against peace.

SPEER
That is a concept taken from civil law and can't be applied to criminal law. The criminal law applies only when the actions carried out favor the realization of punishable acts. This is not this case.

FISCAL
Did the war take you by surprise? Everyone saw it coming, except you.

SPEER

Hitler public speeches did not allow us to guess he had plans for an aggressive war. When Germany signed the non-aggression pact with Russia, it was a great relief because eliminated the perspective of war. Unfortunately, it was not so. Those who signed the pact had also read MY FIGHT, and yet negotiated the pact with the Russians. And they were certainly much smarter than me in political matters.

FISCAL

Let us clarify this point. Do you claim that you did not know Hitler's war plans?

SPEER

I didn't know about them. The war was already underway when I accepted the position in the government. Consequently, I cannot be guilty of conspiracy to unleash an aggressive war.

FISCAL

You have stated in previous interrogations that you accepted to be Minister for Armaments and War Production very hesitantly. Could you explain?

SPEER

I had no interest in dealing with arms production. I just wanted, and want to be, an architect. I accepted because Hitler promised me that I would continue to work as an architect in our city remodeling plans after winning the war.

FISCAL

You took charge in February 1942, and by 1943 more than doubled the production of weapons, increased 80%

fighter jets, and the delivery time of submarines for the *Kriegsmarine* was reduced from one year to two months. Tank delivery went from 4,900 to 17,300 units. Production continued to increase until the second half of 1944, when it stagnated and then began to decrease as a result of the bombings. Can you confirm this data?

SPEER

Totally so. I have kept a set of documents with information about the arms industry in a safe in Hamburg to be used as evidence in this trial. I can make the documents available to the Court.

FISCAL

Why did you keep those documents?

SPEER

They could be useful for a possible trial. A few months before the end, we took it for granted that the war was lost and that we should prepare for the aftermath. So, everyone in Germany dedicated their efforts to thinking and implementing post-war plans.

FISCAL

You have been responsible for prolonging the war for two years. If the increase in arms production would have not existed, the war would have lasted much less and millions of lives would have been saved.

SPEER

I did for my country what anyone would have done: my best efforts.

FISCAL
Was the increase in production mainly due to the increase in slave labor?

SPEER
Production increased much more than labor. A large part of the increase in productivity was achieved through organizational and technical measures.

FISCAL
What measures are you talking about exactly?

SPEER
I gave the companies autonomy, increasing their own responsibilities. Each plant was concentrated in a single product, and most importantly. I put specialists in charge, qualified technicians who knew about industrial organization and production, discarding party officials, politicians, bureaucrats. Most of all, without bureaucrats, I have always hated them.

FISCAL
How many workers were under his supervision?

SPEER

The number increased progressively during the war. It reached a maximum of 14 million.

FISCAL
How many were slaves?

SPEER
Hard to tell, but I guess around 7 million

FISCAL
And how many prisoners of war?

SPEER
Around 2 million

FISCAL
Many Jews worked for war industries. Despite this, they were deported and their jobs were to be replaced. You must inevitably have known this.

SPEER
Yes, I knew it.

FISCAL
Then, you knew the fate of the Jews.

SPEER
I did not know. I only knew that losing the workforce harmed the war effort. Every time I protested; Hitler told me that he didn't want the Jews to collaborate with the German war effort, that the Jews should be set apart, even those who agreed willingly to work for us. But I didn't know the final destiny of the Jews. I had no idea they were exterminated.

FISCAL
Does it mean that exterminating the Jews was more important than winning the war?

SPEER
So it was in Germany. I never agreed. From my point of view, the priority was to win the war. And if the Jews were contributing to the war effort, they should be used. If the Jews had remained in their workplaces, it would have been much easier to produce the necessary

armaments. They had a very important role in the war industry. They were very qualified and productive workers.

FISCAL
So, the conclusion is that the extermination of the Jews was the first priority, even more important than winning the war.

SPEER
So it was. There was no rationale in many of Hitler's decisions. That's why we lost the war. Removing Jews from war industries where they were very useful for sending them to concentration camps was an absurd decision, without any logic.

FISCAL
In 1944 about 100,000 Hungarian Jews were deported to work in the underground factories of airplanes and you did not object. Is this correct?

SPEER
Right.

FISCAL
It was done against the will of the workers?

SPEER
Yes, exactly. They were forced.

FISCAL
Therefore, you didn't care about using illegal procedures to get workers for your factories?

SPEER
They were not illegal in Germany. In August 1942 a

Hitler's decree authorized the use of force to recruit workers, in case they didn't agree.

FISCAL
We charge you with criminal offences related to forced deportation, conspiracy, enslavement of foreign labor, illegal use of prisoners of war and lodging them in concentration camps in degrading conditions. These actions are the consequence of the Nazi ideology, which has made force, brutality and terror the instruments of political power. The combination of forced recruitment, assembly line work, degrading housing, poor food, deplorable sanitary conditions, systematic torture and summary executions is inacceptable to the humanity of the twentieth century

SPEER
I admit the facts, but I don't consider myself responsible.

FISCAL
You used foreign workers knowing that they were being forced to work against their will.

SPEER
I always opposed compulsive recruitment, and did my best not to happen. It was not possible to have a good productivity based on forced workers. It just didn't work. That's why I implanted the concept of "blocked industries". Workers who were in factories in their own country could not be forced to work in Germany and manufactured non-military products. The industries that were liberated in Germany could then be dedicated to the production of armaments. In this way, were avoided the acts of violence against the German police executing

forced recruitment and also the development of guerrillas as a means of resistance.

FISCAL

But, nevertheless, you continued with the illegal incorporation of labor against the will of the workers.

SPEER

It was a practice that had already been used by Dr. Todt, my predecessor. It was already in progress when I took over the Ministry. It was not my responsibility to question the legality of the procedures already in place. I had assumed that this issue had already been considered at the time when the decision was made by those who were then responsible.

FISCAL

How was the legality of those procedures justified?

SPEER

I do not know. It should be assumed that the offices that were responsible for mobilizing workers, under the responsibility of Fritz Sauckel, the Plenipotentiary for Personnel Recruitment, had examined in detail the legal basis of their tasks. Sauckel always claimed that the transportation of labor to Germany was carried out strictly within the legal limits. I am not the creator of these practices. I am not responsible for the methods Sauckel used to recruit the workers that I requested

FISCAL

The forced recruitment of workers is a crime against humanity.

SPEER

I was always in favor of using German labor and not having foreign labor. My policy was to use foreign workers in their own country for civil production and generate reserves of German labor to produce armaments in our country.

FISCAL

Describe what actions did you perform in order to achieve that goal.

SPEER

I was always in favor of the integration of women into the war effort. They had to leave their homes to enter the factories and contribute to the war effort. This is what happened in America and England, but Hitler was against it. He did not want the civil population to suffer the ravages of war and harm the basis of his political support. For Hitler, women had to devote themselves to having children and raising them. This is how we had to resort to the recruitment of foreign workers.

FISCAL

The more we know, the more sinister the Nazi regime seems. Did Hitler prefer to recruit foreign slave labor rather than hire his own countrywomen?

SPEER

Exactly, after several attempts and repeated refusals of Hitler and his Ministers, all my efforts were focused on manufacturing consumer and non-war products in France, Belgium, Czechoslovakia and other countries to free German manpower to produce armaments.

FISCAL
Why did you prefer German labor for armaments?

SPEER
There were no language problems, the training period was much shorter, the mortality was much lower, they were much more motivated and consequently had much higher productivity.

FISCAL
Apparently, it was not enough because you continued with the policy of forced recruitment in the civilian population.

SPEER
So it was.

FISCAL
What was your responsibility in recruiting foreign labor?

SPEER
Setting the number of workers required for each manufacturing unit and communicating the requirement to Sauckel. When the workers were delivered, my responsibility was to assign the workers to each unit.

FISCAL
You were then responsible for establishing the number of slaves required by the German war machine, for the use of foreign civilians under inhuman and degrading conditions and prisoners of war for the manufacture of weapons, ammunition, construction of fortifications and even military operations .The use of prisoners of war in actions against their own country is prohibited by the treaty of the Geneva Convention.

SPEER

Prisoners of war were not used in actions against their own country. They were used in support and logistics actions.

FISCAL

Did you know that many of the prisoners who worked as slaves had already the served their sentence and therefore had to be released?

SPEER

Yes, I knew it. I wrote a letter requesting Himmler to release these prisoners, but he didn't. He considered that these prisoners should continue in the so-called *Schutzhaft,* "protective custody".

FISCAL

Clarify to this Court what "protective custody" is.

SPEER

On February 28, 1933, 18 days after the seizure of power, a decree established the *Schutzhaft,* the so-called protective custody, which granted the power to the Gestapo to send people to prison without judicial intervention. The exact phrase was: "Protective custody for the interest of security and public order."

FISCAL

What do you mean by without judicial intervention?

SPEER

Detention was made without trial, without indication of the time it would last and often without accusation. The fate of an individual was subject to the decision of the Police and the head of the concentration camp.

FISCAL

Did you participate in the economic looting of the
occupied territories?

SPEER

I was involved in the economic exploitation of the
occupied territories, but I don't think it was a "looting".

FISCAL

Didn't you import metals from Belgium, France and other
countries to compensate for the lack of raw materials for
the war industry?

SPEER

I did not import myself. I was involved in some way but
without being responsible. My position was that we
should obtain the metals where possible.

FISCAL

What do you consider your level of responsibility in the
forced recruitment and transportation of workers against
your will?

SPEER

I have described my actions. Regarding my degree of
responsibility related to the utilization of forced labor, I
must say that it is up to the Court to make that decision.

FISCAL

Did the conspiracy of the Nazis include the destruction of
entire ethnic groups through labor?

SPEER

Fritz Sauckel was the Federal Nazi Plenipotentiary of
Labor and directed the recruitment, deportation and
assignment of foreign civilian labor

FISCAL

Did he use force and coercion as recruitment
instruments?

SPEER

So it was. I did not agree, but there was nothing I could do
about it.

FISCAL

This whole process was carried out with two goals: to
operate the war industry and at the same time weaken
and exterminate the people considered inferior. In
summary, the Nazi criminal policy could be defined by the
phrase "extermination through work." You were part of
that criminal scheme.

SPEER

The responsibility for the conditions of the workers was
divided between the Ministry of Food, the Minister of
Health, the Minister of the Interior and the Minister
Plenipotentiary for the Use of Labor. I did not have any
authority in this regard.

FISCAL

Is there anyone in the Nazi government responsible for
anything?

SPEER

In the Reich, there was no coordination between
ministries to execute joint policies. Each department head
had autonomy and the conflicts were permanent. My
responsibility was only the production. When my factory
managers complained, I tried my best to solve the
coordination problems. As Minister of Armaments, I did
everything within my power to keep my workers alive. A

high mortality rate was very inconvenient because it decreased productivity and caused many operational problems.

FISCAL

The detention and deportation of slave labor was carried out brutally and untimely in cities and villages, in the street, in the squares, in the stations, and even in the churches. The relatives were ignorant of fate and remained in complete distress. Regardless of their physical situation, age, or any other condition, they were immediately deported to Germany cutting off all their social and family ties. It was the methodology used in the most tragic era of slave hunting in Africa.

SPEER

I had no participation or responsibility in those actions. I never agreed, but I couldn't do anything. It was authorized by Hitler, *Fuhrerprinzip-*

FISCAL

Do you participate in meetings where these decisions were made?

SPEER

I participated expressing my labor needs. My ministry faced huge challenges, especially for the continuous air attacks that destroyed the factories. I could only deal with the elements related to my work, unless unexpected events forced me to divert my attention. Otherwise, I was very happy to continue with my plans and finish my own work.

FISCAL
This Court is not interested if the plans were good or bad,
but if they were legal or illegal.

SPEER
These methods were legal from my point of view and
were in place before I assumed the Ministry. Whether or
not the laws were legal, couldn't be verified at that time
and in those circumstances. Besides, this matter was none
of my business.

FISCAL
It was not just an arms production program using slave
labor from concentration camps, but also an
extermination scheme based on a deliberate lack of food
that inevitably led to the death of workers. The majority
of the German population did not suffer from this lack of
food. Therefore, underfeeding was a deliberate action.

SPEER
The food and the calories provided were was below the
minimum needs of the workers. I did my best with the
Ministry of Food to increase the number of calories per
worker. The results were not satisfactory.

FISCAL
Was the use of workers from concentration camps known
and approved by you?

SPEER
Yes. I did know, but never approved. In my opinion, the
recruitment of workers had to be done on a free will basis.

FISCAL
Have you ever been to any concentration camp?

SPEER

I was once in Mauthausen, but I didn't see anything that caught my attention. They were severe but acceptable conditions. I did not see abuse.

FISCAL

Have you ever been to any death camp?

SPEER

There was no such expression in our language. In our *Amtsprache*, our bureaucratic language, they were known as *Katset*, or *Konzentrationslager*.

FISCAL *(with annoyance)*
Answer the question

SPEER

Karl Hanke, *Gauleiter* of Lower Silesia, recommended that I should never accept an invitation to inspect a concentration camp, since he had seen scenes he was not authorized to describe.

FISCAL

Did he mean Auschwitz?

SPEER

Probably, this *lager* had a bad reputation.

FISCAL

What does the expression "bad reputation" mean? What kind of reputation are you talking about?

SPEER

It's hard to define, but it was well known in Germany that staying in a concentration camp was a very unpleasant experience. I didn't know the details.

FISCAL

Did you know that physical violence was used to impose regulations on the prisoners?

SPEER

I didn't know anything about that kind of violence. As Minister, I based my decisions on reports originating in other Ministries. This was not subject to my direct responsibility.

FISCAL

The use of slave labor and the misuse of prisoners of war make you guilty of crimes against humanity and war crimes. In September 1942 you convinced Hitler that the only way to increase production was by using the prisoners but under your control. The prisoners were under the jurisdiction of the SS. What did Himmler receive in exchange for providing his prisoners?

SPEER

A percentage of the armaments produced with their workforce based on the number of man hours contributed. To reduce transportation costs, we start organizing small concentration camps near factories. Over time we set up a factory near Auschwitz which was called Birkenau.

FISCAL

The concentration camps were the fundamental institution of the Nazi regime. It was the pillar of the terror system by which the Nazis consolidated their power and imposed their ideology on the German people. It was also the main weapon against Jews, dissidents, the Catholic Church, organized workers and against all kind of dissent. The systematic use of terror was necessary to achieve the state of cohesion within Germany required to carry out the plans for an aggressive war. You have been part of this criminal scheme.

SPEER

These practices were already current before I became Minister. Having accepted and continued these procedures does not make me guilty in the field of criminal law, as they apply only in the field of civil law. Criminal law only applies to actions that serve to give rise to circumstances considered punishable.

FISCAL

You have repeatedly stated that you were unaware of the final fate of the Jews. However, there is evidence that you have participated in the Posen conference and heard Himmler's speech. I go on to read Himmler's speech in Posen:" The extermination of the Jewish race is one of those topics easy to talk about. The Jewish race is being exterminated, says a comrade of the party. It is very clear, it is in our program, we are doing it. We are exterminating them. And then, 80.000.000 good Germans come and each one of them has "his decent Jew" Of course, everyone else is poison. But none of them has witnessed. None has gone through the experience of seeing 100 bodies lying next to each other, or 500 or 1000, and despite this, staying decent, showing no weakness, with a few exceptions. These actions have hardened us. It's a page of glory in our history that has never been written, nor will it ever be. Because we know how difficult it has been and continues to be when, despite the bombings and deprivations of war, we still have Jews in each city today who secretly sabotage, agitate the population and cause problems of all kinds. We are the supreme race. We must be tough."

SPEER *(disturbed)*
I have been to the Posen conference. But I had to leave before Himmler's speech and I did not listen to his lecture.

FISCAL
Are there any witnesses of your early departure?

SPEER
Yes. You can talk to Herr Kempf. He was witness.

FISCAL
Did your fellow *Gauleiter* not tell you about the content of the speech?

SPEER
The subject of the final destiny of the Jews was a taboo subject. No one talked about it.

FISCAL
When were you convinced that the war was lost?

SPEER
In January 1945. My main discrepancies with Hitler began when he wanted to apply the scorched earth policy. Hitler wanted to destroy all the facilities before withdrawing the troops: bridges, plants, warehouses, factories, transmission lines, everything. He wanted Germany to go back to the Stone Age and making the survival of the German people impossible. I couldn´t accept such an atrocity. The German people had to survive.

FISCAL
Did you implement the scorched earth policy?

SPEER
In March 1945 Hitler told me that if the war was lost, the

nation must also die. That Germany shouldn´t survive, since our people had proved to be the weakest and the future belonged only to the nations of the East, which had proved to be stronger. That those who kept fighting were inferior human beings and the good ones had already fallen. It was a breaking point of my relationship with Hitler

FISCAL
Did you receive orders to destroy all facilities and infrastructure?

SPEER
Hitler's direct orders: the so-called *Nero-Befhel,* the Decree of Nero.

FISCAL
Disobeying Hitler's orders meant high treason and death penalty. How did he manage to disobey Hitler and stay alive?

SPEER
To begin with, I managed to convince Hitler not to destroy the factories on the grounds that they would be useful in the future when we recapture the territories lost. Hitler nodded in agreement with a gleam of hope in his eyes.

FISCAL
Did you think it was possible to recover the territories?

SPEER
No way. It was just a pretext to get Hitler to approve my proposal, an argument Hitler wanted to believe. But, on March 25, a month before the end, he resumed the idea of the scorched earth policy with a new decree. Hitler

thought that his fate was the same as the fate of the German people. This time I said no, this is not going to happen...

FISCAL
What did you do, then?

SPEER
I disobeyed Hitler's direct orders with grave risk of my life. I have reached my limit. Hitler could not make impossible the survival of our people. It was craziness. I sent several letters to Hitler refusing to comply with the orders. I even issued orders to withdraw the stock of explosives held by the *Gauleiter* and to suspend the production of industrial explosives used in the demolitions. Kehrl, the head of my Commodities Office is a witness.

FISCAL
Why were you not executed?

SPEER
How would I know, maybe because of affection, maybe an outburst of sanity and common sense. Maybe Hitler wanted to fire me, but I couldn't do it. My Ministry was too important

FISCAL
Why was it so important?

SPEER
Without my presence, the government would have collapsed. Germany would have become ungovernable.

FISCAL
Who else agreed with the scorched earth policy?

SPEER
Goebbels and Bormann

FISCAL
The two are dead now.

SPEER
Probably because they were in favor of these measures
and similar ones.

SPEER
Was there any support to the scorched earth policy from
some of the 21 accused by this court?

SPEER
Not that I remember, on the contrary, Funk was totally
against it.

FISCAL
You have been very critical about the people surrounding
Hitler, his intimate group. Who are the persons you would
criticize the most?

SPEER
I will not name them here and now.

FISCAL
Don't you want to name them because there really are no
criticisms?

SPEER
I criticize them, but it doesn't seem right to name them in
these circumstances. Even considering the when I began
to declare that the war was lost, they all stopped greeting
me and withdrew their trust on me.

FISCAL
When did that happen?

SPEER
March 45, I began to declare that the war was lost and
that we should act accordingly.

FISCAL
It was forbidden by law to be pessimistic about the end of
the war. It was a high treason, a crime punishable by
death penalty. What happened to you? You are still alive.

SPEER
I had a meeting on March 29 with Hitler. He told me that I
should assume the consequences if I continued to declare
that the war was lost.

FISCAL
What were the consequences?

SPEER
Court martial and summary execution. I decided to act
according to my own opinions. I always considered my
obligation to be a servant of the people and of the Nation,
without thinking about my personal safety. I acted as I
thought I should act. To believe in the final victory at that
point was insane, as insane as continuing to feed the myth
of secret weapons or to organize the teenagers as a
fighting force called the *Werewolfs.*

FISCAL
How was that myth fed?

SPEER
The Government generated rumors that there were new
weapons in development, miraculous weapons that

without the use of soldiers, without army forces, could achieve victory. This is why so many people in Germany continued to sacrifice their lives, although the most elementary common sense indicated that the war was lost. I wrote to Hitler in various occasions stating that he should not encourage false hopes and thus manipulate the people. But Hitler had taken the position that if he could not survive, he would not care about Germany's fate. He did not want peace negotiations and launched the *"wir geben nicht auf"*, the "we will not give up" propaganda campaign.

FISCAL
Who was in charge of the Werewolves?

SPEER
Martin Bormann, Hitler's private secretary. I always thought that sending boys aged 14 to 16 to fight Russian troops was messianic madness. They were totally unnecessary and useless deaths. It was just another demonic action similar to the destruction of factories and facilities.

FISCAL
Bormann, and who else?

SPEER
As far as I know, only Bormann.

FISCAL
Were you involved in the bomb attack on Hitler led by Colonel von Stauffenberg in July 1944, in the operation called Valkyrie?

SPEER

On the July 1944 putsch, I was on the list as Minister of Armaments of the new government, but without being consulted. I was the only one of Hitler's ministers on that list.

FISCAL

Why were you not consulted? It was known that you were not happy with the course of events.

SPEER

My loyalty to Fuehrer was out of the question, despite my discrepancies. Everyone knew that. After the coup, the Nazis made an investigation and a list appeared in which my name had a question mark and a hand written no "persuade", a detail that saved me from the extensive purges of the regime that followed the plot.

FISCAL

Would you have participated in the putsch if you had been contacted?

SPEER

In July 1944 no, my fidelity to Fuehrer prevailed. From January 1945, when I was convinced that the war was lost, I considered the idea of throwing poisonous gas through a vent of the bunker. But such an action could not be carried out without killing the other inhabitants of the bunker. It was too many lives, too many innocents. I couldn't do it.

FISCAL

On April 23, a week before the end, you flew in a small light plane to see Hitler again. What important matters led you to take such great risks as landing in Berlin when the city was already fighting the Russians on the streets?

SPEER

I wanted to greet Fuehrer for the last time and express my personal support.

FISCAL

Some rumors circulate that you went to talk to Hitler to convince him not to be named as his successor, because this would have jeopardized your chances of participating in Germany's restoration efforts after the end of the war.

SPEER

That is not true. I was never considered a successor. I was not even mentioned in his will.

FISCAL

It is this total absence in the will that fuels this version. You were always mentioned as Hitler's probable successor.

SPEER

I repeat it again: This rumor is just a rumor, it is not correct. Admiral Karl Dönitz was always the best candidate.

FISCAL

We can see the same pattern on all the testimonies of the defendants: Nobody knew anything about what was happening, but they did know that the responsibility was someone else's. Preferably from a colleague who is already dead or missing. All these men saw nothing wrong, said nothing bad or nothing bad was said in their presence. Are you willing to assume some kind of responsibility?

SPEER

This war has brought about a terrible European and world catastrophe. Consequently, it is my duty to assume my share of responsibility for this disaster before the German people. As a member of the Reich government since 1942, I have a participation in the responsibility, collectively but not individually.

FISCAL

When you refer to shared responsibility, do you assume a crime under criminal law, or do you simply want to leave for the record a historical responsibility toward your own people?

SPEER

It is a difficult question to answer. This Court will decide my degree of responsibility. I want to say that even in authoritarian societies; leaders must accept a common responsibility and it´s impossible, after a catastrophe, to avoid it. If the war had been won, those same leaders would have claimed total responsibility for the victory. But to what extent this responsibility is punishable or immoral, I can´t decide. It is up to this Court.

FISCAL

Does your so-called collective responsibility include the extermination of the Jews?

SPEER

I am not personally responsible for the extermination, but I am collectively responsible because I was part of a government whose policy was the destruction of the Jews by physical means.

FISCAL

Why didn't you quit the government when you
understood the nature of Hitler's regime?

SPEER

In war times it was very difficult to see things clearly. I
saw destruction, corpses, deportations, but the picture
was fuzzy. I should have asked Himmler or Hitler about
what was happening in the concentration camps. I
consider this oversight the most important failure of my
life.

FISCAL

So, you admit shared responsibility but not personal?
What do you mean exactly by shared responsibility?

SPEER

A State official has two responsibilities. One is the
personal responsibility for its own sector and the other is
the shared responsibility for being part of a government
with certain essential values that are common to the
entire State. This shared responsibility applies to the
fundamental issues, to the big policies and not to the
operational details of each Ministry

FISCAL

When you knew that the war was lost, you stayed. Not
only stayed, but worked, planned and supported the
regime until the end. How can you explain his behavior?
How can you justify it?

SPEER

I am responsible, not guilty. I did the same as all Germans.
Didn't find out. Didn't know. Didn't want to know. Just
tried to go ahead and keep living. I could have known, I

could have found out, but I decided not to because knowing would have made it impossible for me to move on. I just couldn't do it.

FISCAL
How can there be responsibility without guilt?

SPEER
Guilt must be personal. I am collectively responsible, because I have been part of the government.

FISCAL
You're trying to prove that you are only a technocrat, without responsibility for the policies of the Nazi government, an amoral technocrat. You have expressed your desire to cooperate by providing all kinds of information about the armaments industry and the damage caused by strategic bombings. You have emphasized your opposition to Hitler's scorched earth policy, denied your knowledge of the crimes perpetrated against the Jews and finally attempted to separate himself from the other prisoners based on your personality and degree of guilt. Does this statement reflect your position?

SPEER
Yes, it does.

FISCAL
You have been a blind man, blind by choice. Not ignorant, not immoral, not amoral, but morally exhausted

SPEER
I am an artist, forced against my wishes to participate in political and war activities, trapped because of my duties

towards my homeland and sustained on Hitler's promise to return to architecture after the war.

FISCAL

Your real tragedy is that you didn't care which side you were with, as long as you could benefit. If you could choose between a normal architect's life, build a school per year, family houses, design landscapes and so on, or being Hitler's architect, what would you have chosen?

FISCAL

It's hard to say now when everything has already been left behind. I only hope that this trial serves as a warning to all the Albert Speers who live among us, so that these tragedies won´t happen again.

BLACKOUT

JUDGE (*voiceover*)

This Court considers that the defendant is not guilty of the charge of conspiracy to carry out an aggressive war and the execution of crimes against peace because they were already in progress when he entered the government. This court declares guilty the defendant for war crimes and crimes against humanity and is sentenced to 20 years in prison. The great danger of Albert Speer is that, unlike the other Nazis, he did not join the movement by idealism, but by opportunism. In this age when success, power and status are considered the only worthwhile attributes, his example is really dangerous. The true lesson this trial leaves us is to recognize the Albert Speers who live among us, those who are willing to sell their soul to the Devil every time a Mephistopheles appears with a tempting offer.

THE END